Ulrich Hub

Duck's Backyard

Illustrated by Jörg Mühle
Translated by Helena Kirkby

GECKO PRESS

The goal is in the way

It all begins in a lonely backyard where the sun never shines. Here lives a duck with a wonky leg. She never has any visitors. She has a small supply of peanuts which she'd love to share with someone. But who would choose to set foot in such a gloomy place?

The duck has occasionally thought about venturing into the world outside, but there's always a reason not to. So as not to seize up, she takes a daily walk around the yard with her crutch.

How surprised she is when, one day, someone comes around the corner.

A chicken wearing dark glasses. The duck watches with interest as the chicken wanders

aimlessly around until she finally trips over the
duck's crutch.

"How nice to meet you." The duck politely helps
the dazed chicken back to her feet. "It's gratifying
to meet someone worse off than oneself."

"What do you mean?" the chicken asks in a
surprisingly firm voice. "I'm perfectly all right.
What makes you think there's something wrong
with me?"

"Well, you are blind." The duck sighs. "I can't think of anything worse than being unable to see."

"It doesn't make me any less of a chicken." The chicken laughs. Then she wags her wing. "Being blind has more advantages than you might think. For starters, it means I don't care what you look like—"

The duck's eyes start to blaze. "I don't look too bad, for a duck with a wonky leg—"

"Or if the lights go out in the stairwell and everyone starts to panic," the chicken goes on, unruffled, "I remain completely calm. But the best thing about me is that I'm a remarkably good listener." She stops. "What did you just say?"

"That I look pretty good for a duck with a wonky leg. What's more, I'm loyal, honest and adventurous, and my heart's in the right place—"

"So, you're a duck with a wonky leg!" The chicken quickly stretches her wings and

9

examines the duck from head to toe, then pats her on the head. "I wanted a guide dog, but a duck with a wonky leg is better than nothing. You'll do just as well to guide me on my journey."

At the very thought of leaving her yard, the duck begins to tremble. "I'd need to know where we'd be going."

"Somewhere in the world," the chicken murmurs, "there's a place where all our secret wishes come true. Are you coming?"

"I'll have to think about it."

The duck pokes at the ground with her crutch. It's not the first she's heard of this place. Many have set out in search of it, but all have failed. Nobody has ever found it. It probably doesn't even exist.

"Are you still there?" asks the chicken.

"I'm still thinking."

"Take your time. But get a move on."

"I have a much better idea," says the duck at last. "Why don't we just stay here in my backyard? The outside world is riddled with dangers. It's all too easy to come to a sticky end. We'd be better off making ourselves comfortable here, behind these high walls."

The chicken yawns loudly. Then she comes closer to the duck—maybe a little too close—lays a wing over her shoulder and whispers beguilingly, "Don't you have a secret wish? Come on, you can tell me. Everyone has them."

The duck gulps and feels herself going pink beneath her feathers.

Fortunately, the chicken can't see it.

"My wish will probably never come true." The duck sighs deeply. "I'll come with you, though. Without my help, you'll end up in the nearest ditch, and I'll blame myself forever. In which direction is this place?"

"No idea," says the chicken. "But I'll know once I'm there. The main thing is to get started."

"Without me!" The duck promptly backs off. "I'm not just marching off into the blue. How are we supposed to find this place? We'll only get lost, or drowned, or frozen to death—"

"One thing is for sure," says the chicken. "If we stay here talking, we'll never find it. Let's get out of this gloomy yard! You keep an eye out for me, and I'll prop you up." She grasps the duck energetically under the wing and declares: "We'll get along splendidly. I just know it.

I spread sunshine wherever I go, while you're
as damp as a dishrag."

Every journey begins with a single step.

Very cautiously, the duck sets down one flat
foot, then pauses. She slowly sets down the other
foot and pauses again.

"What's with the snail's pace?" the chicken
asks. "We'll never get there like this. Can't you go
faster?"

"You have a lot to learn," the duck says mildly,
shuffling forwards. "A duck with a limp can't be

expected to hurry. The quickest way to anywhere is by small steps."

Before long, she stops again.

"I'm afraid we'll have to turn back," she says. "I've just remembered I left my crutch in the backyard."

"Back?" the chicken gasps. "Not a chance." She then hits her head with her wing. "Why didn't I think of it sooner? We can just fly! We'll be there in no time."

The duck shakes her head and shuffles on. "I'm opposed to flying. On principle. If you fly, you lose perspective, and have no chance to admire the charming scenery."

"I can't see anything anyway," the chicken mutters.

"We've been walking along a dusty country road," the duck says. "It goes dead straight to the horizon. On the left are a few stunted bushes—"

"Have you ever tried flying?"

"And to the right are trees charred by fire.
The sky above is darkening. I hope the weather
goes on being kind to us—"

"Have you ever even tried?" the chicken asks.

"No," says the duck. "And so what? Flying's too
dangerous for me. If this pace doesn't suit, find
yourself a guide dog."

For a while, there's an uneasy silence. Irked,
the chicken lets herself be led by the duck, with
only the shuffle of flat feet to be heard. But she
can't stand it for long. "Shall I tell you a secret?
Listen—"

"Hang on—not so fast," says the duck. "I need
to know first if it's a big secret or a little one.
And how long I'd have to keep it to myself.
Keeping a secret can be very stressful. If you've
robbed a bank, for example, I'll have to tell the
police your secret. It would be my duty."

"Oh stop being such a fusspot." The chicken's feathers are starting to become ruffled. "I only wanted to tell you my secret wish—"

"Don't bother," the duck replies. "I already know your wish. You wish you could see again."

"Wrong!" the chicken squawks. "If I could see, I'd be just like all the other chickens. But I'm special. That's why my secret wish is so special. It takes a while to come up with something like this. I've thought about it long and hard—"

"Oh, cut out the drama." The duck can't help being a little curious, though. "What is your wish?"

"To enjoy myself and have everyone dance to my tune." The chicken fluffs her feathers. "What do you say to that?"

The duck stares at the chicken. What on earth has she got herself into? She's never heard such a stupid wish in her life.

"Are you still there?" The chicken gropes around for the duck. "Tell me. What do you think of my wish?"

"First, it's two wishes," says the duck. "And second—"

"Know-it-all!" the chicken snaps.

"And second—" the duck is a little shrill. "Why should everyone do what *you* want them to? And by the way, I'm not used to being spoken to in that tone."

"You can be grateful anyone's speaking to you at all, you big wet sponge! Now you tell me your secret wish."

"Huh. Not likely."

"But that's not fair!" the chicken says. "I told you mine!"

"I didn't ask you to!"

"If only I'd found myself a guide dog."

"I said you should've."

And thus they bicker their way at snail's pace until the chicken groans in despair: "We're just talking the whole time, with nothing actually happening. If only we could meet someone for a change. A fox or something. I was expecting a bit more action—"

Next moment, the duck stops so abruptly the chicken clatters into her and goes head over heels.

"What was that about?" she asks, picking herself up.

"I stopped just in time," says the duck. "There's a huge black forest up ahead. It'll be as dark as the belly of a whale in there. We'll have to go around the outside."

"Around the outside? Around the entire forest? That's a senseless detour!"

The chicken marches coolly on. Forget that duck. They'll never get there by making detours. A few moments later, she hears the duck hobbling breathlessly after her.

"Wait for me!" gasps the duck. "Not so fast. Looks like I'm coming with you. Although it's pure madness—"

Then she grips the chicken's wing and leads cautiously on. "We're entering the dark forest now," she says. "Do as I say. If we stray from the path, we'll never find our way out again."

The duck solicitously points out sharp stones and roots; warns of rotten branches that might fall; teaches the chicken about fungi and berries that mustn't be eaten; cringes from ghostly spiders' webs; describes in dismal tones the gnarled trees with trunks overgrown by strange mossy lichens; and is vexed by discarded plastic that could injure wildlife.

"Stop jabbering," says the chicken. "And get a move on."

"I'd like to," the duck wails. "But I can't see a wing in front of my face. The last bit of daylight has gone, and we're completely lost. This is the darkest forest in the world. There's nothing around us but darkest darkness."

"Darkness, my clawed foot. Onwards!" the chicken orders. "And don't go pretending you're tired."

But there is something strange about this forest. Even the chicken has to admit it.

Not a bird is singing in the branches, not a brook is babbling, not the faintest breeze rustles the leaves.

"Peculiar," says the chicken, listening. "It's as quiet as your backyard."

"My backyard?" The duck begins to cry bitter tears. "I want to go home. Why did I let you talk me into this? My yard was my heaven! And I'll never see it again. If only I'd listened to my own duckish good sense—"

"Be quiet!" hisses the chicken.

Thuds are coming from somewhere.

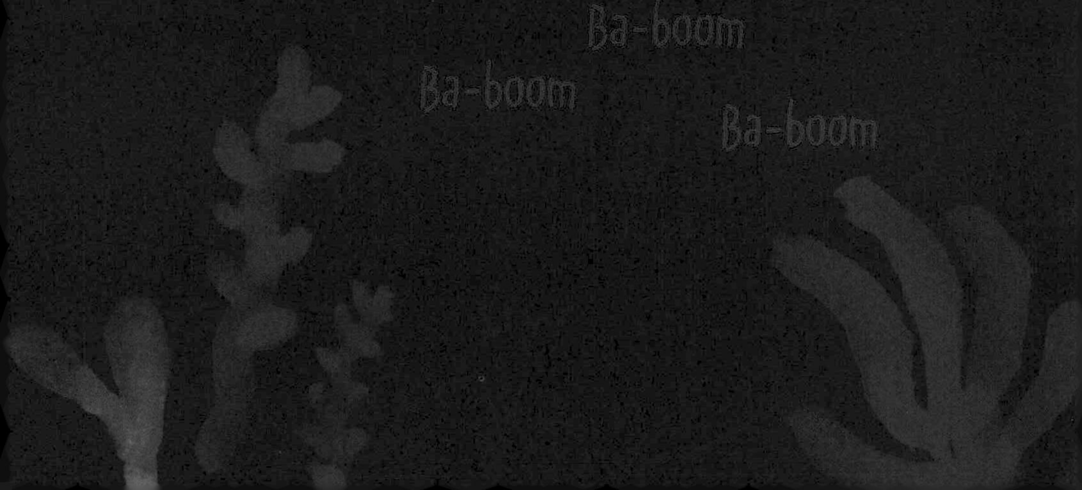

Ba-boom

Ba-boom

Ba-boom

"What's that?" cries the duck.

Ba-boom   Ba-boom   Ba-boom

"This is the end of me!" the duck shrieks and
she flings herself flat on the ground with her
wings over her head.

The chicken runs nervously around, listening.
The thuds grow fainter, then louder again. The
chicken leans warily over the duck.

BA-BOOM!
BA-BOOM!
BA-BOOM!

"It's your heart!" the chicken says scornfully.
"Banging like a drum. For goodness' sake, pull
yourself together. You're not a duckling anymore."
Mercilessly, the chicken pulls the duck up.
"Hang on to my shoulders. From now on, I'm in
charge. I can't see a thing anyway."

To avoid bushes, trees and other obstacles,
the chicken flaps her wings like windscreen
wipers, while the duck stumbles along behind her.

"Nothing frightens me as much as the dark.
I have a little nightlight in my yard."

The chicken laughs. "Wasn't it pitch-dark when
you were curled up in your egg?"

"How should I know?" the duck replies from
behind. "No one remembers the time before they
were born."

"I do," says the chicken. "And I've never been so
bored since. I kept wondering who'd put me in
that stupid egg. It was roomy enough, but any
time I wriggled around, someone would knock
on the shell."

"At some point," she continued, "I just had to get out, and couldn't wait until I was bigger. So I gave the shell a kick, a gentle one, but it cracked. Then the crack grew wider and wider, and I was looking into bright light. It was so frightfully bright, I screwed my eyes shut, and when I tried to open them again—"

"Everything stayed black," the duck says.

"How did you know?"

"Common sense. You looked out too soon and spoiled the surprise. You went blind as a punishment."

At once, the duck is ashamed. It's wrong to make a blind chicken think it's her own fault. She resolves to make up for it as soon as possible.

Fortunately, she doesn't have to wait long for an opportunity.

"What do my aching eyes see?" cries the duck in astonishment. "Is that daylight? You've actually led us out of the darkest forest in the world. Without bumping into a single tree. It's almost a miracle. You deserve a reward—"

The chicken hears the duck rustling around.

"What are you up to?" she asks.

"Wait and see. Now. Open your beak."

The chicken doesn't have to be told twice. She opens her beak as wide as she can and feels the duck tipping something into it.

The chicken chomps greedily, smacking her beak, then stops, startled. This was the last thing she expected.

"Peanuts!" she crows. "The snack I love most! How did you conjure those up?"

"I think of everything!" The duck goes on pouring peanuts into the chicken.

"I wish I'd remembered my crutch," she suddenly says, sadly. "I took it for a turn around

the backyard every day, and now it's lying there all alone."

"I'm sure someone will find it who needs it more than you do," says the chicken, crunching peanuts. "You no longer need a crutch. You have me now."

She burps loudly.

The duck is touched, and again feels herself going pink beneath her feathers. Not for the first time, she's glad the chicken can't see her.

They sit munching with gusto on the roasted peanuts, until they're so full they can hardly move.

"Are you going to tell me your secret wish now?" asks the chicken.

"No," says the duck.

"Why not?"

"Because then it won't be a secret."

"That's not true!" says the chicken. "If you tell me your wish, it's still a secret. A shared secret, and only if—"

"We're having such a pleasant rest here at the edge of the forest," says the duck. "Let's not talk for a change, and just enjoy the blissful silence."

"But I have a right to know!" the chicken says. "I led you out of this great dark forest!"

"Without you, I wouldn't have entered the great dark forest in the first place."

The chicken jumps up and stamps her feet. "I know nothing about you, while you know everything about me! Even the bit before I was born. I don't go telling any old duck that kind of thing!" She clenches her wings into fists, and stomps towards the duck. "If you don't tell me your secret wish right this minute, I'll turn you to pulp! I'll beat the secret out of you!"

The duck ducks aside and the chicken flies right past her.

"Where've you gone?" The chicken rushes about like an angry, bristling broom, until at last she has to stop for a breather. "You're only making it worse for yourself," she gasps. "I'll give you such a punishment, you'll wish you'd never been born." Glowing with rage, she roars: "You're—not—coming—to—my—birthday!!"

"Stop!" yells the duck. "You're right on the edge of a cliff!"

She lunges at the chicken and flings her to the ground with such force they both go tumbling, over and over.

"Phew!" gasps the duck. "That was close. There's a huge ravine right behind you."

"A ravine?" The chicken is delighted. "Why didn't you say so? That means we're nearly there!"

She picks herself up, dusts off her feathers, and straightens her dark glasses. "We can simply fly straight over it."

"Too dangerous." The duck folds her wings across her breast. "Flying has many hazards. Ducks are always falling from the sky. Which is something nobody talks about."

The chicken is tired of the duck's excuses. She just needs a bit of instruction. Fortunately, she has the right teacher. There's nobody more experienced or patient than the blind chicken.

"I'll give you a quick demonstration," she says. "There's no particular art to flying. Just don't overthink it."

She stands in front of the duck, legs apart and wings outspread. "Are you watching?"

"Yes." The duck watches as the chicken flaps and puffs and hops, faster and faster, from foot to foot.

"At first, you feel like a rocket about to take off," she cries. "Starting takes the most energy—" She topples and lands with a...

BUMP

"That was only a test flight,"
she mutters.
The duck feels it's best to
say nothing.
The chicken picks herself up,
spreads her wings, and tells
the duck to watch.
Then she flaps and puffs and
hops from foot to foot, and
cries: "I feel like a rocket about
to take off—" Then she falls
over again with a...

BUMP

This time the duck
can't resist.
"Another cancelled
flight," she says.
"Only because you
were watching," snaps
the chicken.
"I'll show you again. But this
time you mustn't watch.
Promise?"

The duck promises
solemnly, squeezes her eyes
shut, and hears the chicken
flap and puff and hop and...

BUMP

She opens her eyes to see the chicken in a heap on the ground.

"Nothing like this has ever happened before," the chicken mutters, embarrassed. "It's all your fault. Those pesky peanuts are weighing me down. I hope I've not put on any weight."

The duck is secretly pleased to be spared the flight. "Your figure is in great shape. You're just tired from the long journey. Why not have a nap?"

"I'm not even tired," the chicken moans.
"It's all so unfair. First, I don't get a guide dog
but a gloomy duck—a consolation prize—then
the rocket doesn't work, and now I'm supposed to
go to sleep when I'm not even tired. There's only
one thing I wish for in the whole world. I wish…"
She pauses. "What's my secret wish again?"

"You can't have forgotten that." The duck
chuckles.

"Stop that stupid giggling," snaps the chicken,
"and try to help me. At least give me a clue."

"Tune," the duck whispers.

"For everyone to dance to my tune," the chicken
says triumphantly. "Right?"

"Wrong," says the duck. "You forgot the first
bit. To enjoy myself and—"

The chicken starts to cry. "To enjoy myself
and for everyone to dance to my tune. To enjoy
myself—" Fat tears roll from under her glasses.
"Boo-hoo! How could I have forgotten?

I never forget anything. Boo-hoo! Show me one
other chicken who can remember the time before
they were born." She wipes away her tears.
"I might be a tiny bit overtired—"

She rolls onto her side, sniffs, and softly begins
to snore.

The duck looks at the sleeping chicken with a
smile. She kneels down and takes her head in
her lap.

"Am I too fat?" the chicken asks suddenly.

The duck gives a start. "I thought you were
asleep."

"Am I too fat?"

"You're just right for me."

"So, I'm too fat," the chicken growls. Then her breathing becomes calm and even.

The duck is starting to enjoy the silence when the chicken asks: "How do I look when I'm asleep?"

The duck takes a deep breath. "I'm afraid I can't tell you."

"Why not?"

"Because you never go to sleep!" A duck can lose her patience.

"How can anyone get to sleep with all this racket?" the chicken mumbles, and then she snores gently again.

The chicken has no idea how long she's been asleep when she is rudely shaken awake.

"Wake up, sleepyhead," the duck quacks. "Rise and shine. I have great news."

The chicken rolls over with a grunt. What kind of news can the dishrag possibly have?

"While you slept, I was not idle," the duck declares. "I scouted around and came across a plank. I laid it across the ravine like a bridge, so now we can walk over."

The chicken has never got up so quickly. She wants to be led straight to the ravine and is about to march over when the duck stops her.

"Let me go first. I need to check that the plank will hold us both."

Trembling, she puts one flat foot on it. "Don't push me," she snaps. "You can follow, but hold on tight. The plank is terribly narrow. One false step and we plunge to the depths."

With knocking knees, the duck sets out. "Whatever happens, I mustn't look down. I'm already dizzy. There's a wild mountain river far below us, with brown water rushing and hurtling around boulders."

"Strange." The chicken puts her wings round the duck's middle and follows her. "I can't hear any rushing or hurtling."

"Because we're too far above it," says the duck in a trembling voice. "This is the deepest ravine in the world."

"But I have acute hearing, and—"

"I'm concentrating on this narrow plank," the duck says crossly. "I mustn't be distracted by unnecessary comments."

"If we fall into the water," the chicken says carelessly, "we'll just swim."

"Be my guest," the duck retorts. "You only have to let go of me. But I'll tell you this much: the water down there is freezing. Your heart would shrink to an ice cube. You'd swallow heaps of water; you'd have a coughing fit and run out of air. Then you'd flap your wings in a panic, your feathers would soak up water, and you'd sink like a stone."

The chicken has already slowed down, her wings wrapped as tight as can be around the duck's middle.

"But probably you wouldn't even land in water," the duck hisses. "You'd land on a rock. And go as flat as a pancake—"

"A pancake?!"

Alarmed, the chicken lets go of the duck, wobbles, loses her balance, flaps her wings so hectically that she loses a few feathers—and at the last moment, feels the duck grabbing her.

"Have you gone mad?" shrieks the duck. "You almost pulled me down with you!"

The chicken is so shocked that she has rolled herself into a formless bundle of feathers and can't move, however hard she tries.

She is paralyzed by fear.

"Look, I know how you feel," says the duck in a desperate voice. "But we can't stay hovering here between Heaven and Earth!"

The duck changes tone and speaks to the chicken with the gentle tongue of an angel, reminding her of all she's achieved in her life.

"All alone, you crept from your egg; as a blind chick, you've been halfway around the world without ending up in a ditch; you spread sunshine wherever you go, and you only need to take these last few steps..."

The chicken doesn't budge.

"But your greatest achievement so far," says the duck, swallowing hard, "was convincing a damp old dishrag like me to get going."

"True." The chicken is emerging from her paralysis. She takes a tentative step. "That was my masterstroke. If only you knew how often I've regretted it, though. It really is punishing to travel with a duck like you. You're never satisfied—"

"You're doing well," says the duck. "Very nearly there—"

"You always look on the dreary side." The chicken is moving a little faster. "You burst into tears at the first opportunity. You're boring, awkward, opinionated, and you don't smell all that good—"

"Only a couple more steps," the duck says in a tight voice, as the chicken speeds up.

"You ought to have a good wash when you get the chance. Someone should have told you years ago—only you don't have any friends, which isn't surprising when you go around

smelling of that gloomy yard. But the worst
thing about you is—"

"Keep note of it," the duck says quickly, "and
tell me later. We've made it. What a relief!"

At first, the chicken can hardly believe it.
She stamps left, then right, and when she feels
solid ground all around, she jumps for joy.
"I survived! We made it over the deepest ravine in
the world! This calls for a celebration! Let's dance!"

"Dance?" The duck winces.

She's never done anything so crazy. She doesn't know how to. She'd be bound to embarrass herself. Should she risk it?

At least there's nobody watching. The duck takes a deep breath, screws up her courage and, concentrating hard, juts out her right hip.

Then she carefully shoves her bottom out the other way and starts to gently sway.

A joint makes a soft crack. The duck hears it with horror. Luckily, nothing hurts. She feels herself grow bolder—almost cocky— and she does a tiny hop.

"Brilliant. Quite brilliant," says the chicken, clapping her wings in delight. "I can't

see you,
but you're
dancing like
a little elf!
I feel it in
my bones."
She grabs the
surprised duck,
who yelps with
delight, and together
they twirl around.
The dance

grows fast and exuberant,
with duck and chicken
clasped together, and
goes on merrily until
they both drop into
an exhausted heap.

There they lie snuggled close—perhaps a little too close—and the duck once again feels herself turn pink under her feathers. But the chicken also seems a little bashful.

"I never imagined," says the duck at last, quietly, "that dancing could be so much fun."

The chicken gives the duck a dig in the ribs. "Now you can tell me your secret wish."

"Maybe later—"

"What are you so afraid of?" the chicken persists. "You don't have to be embarrassed with me. We can tell each other anything, can't we?"

"Well, you mustn't laugh at me." The duck takes a deep breath. "It's not that I want to fly, and my wonky leg doesn't bother me—"

"I'd already worked that out."

"My secret wish is—" the duck murmurs, then she pauses.

"Tell me!" The chicken pokes the duck in the ribs again. "It'll make you feel better. Just say it!"

The pressure is too much for the duck, and she moves away.

"Are you still there?" asks the chicken.

"Where do you think I am? But I'd rather not tell you my wish. Every duck has the right to a little secret."

Disappointed, the chicken gets up.

"Tell you what, then." She smooths her ragged feathers. "I don't want to know your secret wish. It's probably completely stupid anyway."

"However stupid my wish might be," says the duck, "it won't be as stupid as yours."

"What do you mean?" asks the chicken. "What's so stupid about wishing for—" She pauses. "What's my secret wish?"

The duck rolls her eyes. "Have you forgotten again?"

"Give me a clue."

"Your secret wish," the duck whispers, "includes the word 'tune'."

"Is this some kind of puzzle?" The chicken scratches her head. Then she fires it out: "For everyone to dance to my tune! Right?"

"Almost," says the duck. "You forgot the first bit again. Your secret wish is: 'To enjoy myself and for everyone to dance to my tune.'"

"Enjoy," the chicken says sullenly. "That's what I said. You don't listen properly. I'm beginning to wonder who I am. We need to make a move. The more time I fritter away with you, the less I can remember my own wish."

As they walk along, the chicken mutters her secret wish over and over, until all the words run together.

Toenjoymyselfandforeveryonetodanceto
mytunetoenjoymyselfandforeveryonetodance
tomytuneToenjoymyselfandforeveryonetodancetomy
tunetoenjoymyselfandforeveryonetodancetomytune
Toenjoymyselfandforeveryonetodancetomytunetoenjoy
myselfandforeveryonetodancetomytuneToenjoymyselfandfor
everyonetodancetomytuneToenjoymyselfandforeveryonetodanceto
mytunetoenjoymyselfandforeveryonetodancetomytuneToenjoymyself
andforeveryonetodancetomytunetoenjoymyselfandforeveryone todance
tomytuneToenjoymyselfandforeveryonetodancetomytunetoenjoymyselfandfor
everyone todancetomytuneToenjoymyselfandforeveryonetodancetomytunetomytuneto
enjoymyselfandforeveryonetodance...

"Who actually is this *everyone?*" the duck interrupts. "I've been wondering all along."

"Everyone in the whole world."

"What?!" For a few moments, the duck is speechless. "Why should the whole world dance to the tune of a chicken in dark glasses?"

"Because I know what's best for everyone," says the chicken. "I go around spreading sunshine. Look at you, for example. Before we met, you were a duck with a wonky leg. You still have a wonky leg, but at least you're no longer—"

"Damp as a dishrag," the duck says pertly.

"Shut your beak," the chicken snaps. "I'm trying to learn my secret wish off by heart so I can recite it flawlessly when I get there." She pauses. "How does it begin, again?"

The duck slams to a halt and before the chicken can complain, she declares solemnly: "A huge, steep mountain looms before us, crowned by a lonely and majestic peak." She lowers her voice. "It's the highest mountain in the world, and nobody has ever reached its summit."

"How do you know?"

"It says so on a sign."

"So you can read," the chicken laughs scornfully. "But when it comes to flying—"

"Reading is easy. Flying is difficult," says the duck, craning her head back. "I hope you're not thinking of climbing this. Mountains are not to be trifled with. It's freezing up there. The air is thin. We're completely unequipped for such an expedition with our light plumage. We'd end up dead."

The chicken fidgets with excitement. The goal is within their grasp! All they have to do is climb the highest mountain in the world.

"Happiness lies at the summit!"

But the duck droops her head.

"I'm afraid you'll have to go up alone," she says. "My leg has been bothering me all along, and dancing with you— although I loved it—rather finished me off." She sighs audibly. "I'm done in. You'd have to carry me, and I can't ask that of you. I'm far too heavy."

"Don't be silly," says the chicken. "You're as light as a feather."

And like a true hero, she heaves her exhausted comrade onto her shoulders. The chicken is impressed by her own bravery. Not long ago she was wanting a guide dog, and now here she is, piggybacking a duck.

She probably deserves a medal for this.

"We're getting higher and higher," says the duck. "Fir branches hang heavy in the damp air. Wild and threatening cliffs rise around us. The forests are already far below, and thick clouds roll through the valley—"

"The ground feels flat to me," the chicken says in surprise. "Are we really going uphill?"

"Haven't you noticed how cold it's growing?" The duck chatters her beak. "We're trudging through endless snow—"

"Funny. I'm not the slightest bit cold."

"Because you're carrying me, chickadee," the duck chatters on. "I can barely see a thing now. There's only whiteness all around. This is where pure Nothingness begins—"

The chicken is losing track of up and down. In fact, everything is going topsy-turvy. It must be the thin air up here. She staggers, she sways…

And then she collapses under her burden.

The duck rolls to one side and pleads: "Leave me, just leave me here. You must go on without me. A courageous blind chicken like you deserves to reach the top. My journey ends here, but for you, the fulfilment of your wish awaits—"

"No!" The chicken beats her breast in despair. "It's all my fault! I'm the hapless bird who persuaded you to come on this journey. If it weren't for me, you'd still be in your backyard—"

"Don't blame yourself," the duck whispers. "I don't regret leaving my home for you, not for a single moment." After these words, she folds her wings across her breast and says calmly, "Dying isn't so bad. I have only one last request—"

The chicken can hardly hold back her tears. "I'll do anything you want. Anything."

"Erect a small, simple wooden plaque at the wayside," the duck breathes. "That's all I want. And write on it—"

Her voice falters.

"What?" The chicken bends over her. "Speak louder—"

The duck wheezes. "Urrgghhh..."

"I don't understand. What should it say on the plaque?"

The duck rears up once more and cries with the last of her strength: "Here—lies—a—duck with a wonky leg!"

Then her head drops into the chicken's lap.

The chicken sobs in dismay. "A paltry wooden plaque? You deserve better than that. I'll throw a funeral for you that'll be talked about for centuries. I give you my solemn vow. With flowers and wreaths and marching bands, so everyone can see how much I loved you, how very much—"

The duck has never heard such beautiful words in her life. She can't leave them unanswered. Even if it makes her death drawn out. Like in an opera.

"Only once in my life have I been so happy," says the duck, smiling faintly. "In my egg. That's why I never wanted to leave it. The larger I grew, the smaller I folded myself, until I lost all feeling in one leg—but then one day there was a crack—" The duck is almost singing. "The delicate shell cracked, a golden shimmer penetrated my darkness and I looked into the light—"

The duck has been rising imperceptibly and is shaking out her feathers. "Where am I?" She goes on in a surprisingly clear voice. "I can't believe my eyes. The fog has lifted. We're on top of the highest mountain in the world. What a view! We've made it! If only you could see it, chickadee."

It takes a while for the chicken to catch up. "You didn't die?" she says. "You're still alive?"

"Alive and well," the duck exults, and she takes the chicken by the shoulder. "But that's not all. Turn around. There's another surprise for you."

"What? What is it?" stammers the chicken. "Tell me! What are you looking at?"

"You're standing before a colossal archway of pure gold," the duck declares. "Studded with thousands of diamonds and sparkling gemstones."

The chicken clasps her heart and hardly dares to breathe. After all the detours and obstacles, ups and downs, she has finally reached her destination. "I'd given up all hope," she sighs with emotion.

"What are you waiting for? Go on through the archway and state your secret wish."

"Don't I have to wait to be summoned?" asks the chicken. "Or use some kind of code?"

The duck gives her a gentle push. "This entrance was made just for you."

The chicken feels as if she has gone to paradise. It even seems she can hear bells ringing somewhere. Breathless and elated, she takes a step with folded wings—

And then another step—

She stops suddenly, her wings droop, and she looks around for the duck. "What's my secret wish again?"

"I don't believe it!" The duck slaps her forehead. "You can't seriously have forgotten again? How many times did we go over it?"

"I don't suppose you remember, though?" the chicken says in a small voice.

But this time, unfortunately, the duck can't help, however hard she tries. She can't even remember how it begins.

"Please try," begs the chicken. "Even one word of it!"

"Something about—" the duck thinks hard. "The moon?"

"What?" The chicken flops down in despair. "Moon makes no sense. Oh, why can't I remember my own wish?"

"Maybe it's no longer important."

"What do you mean?"

"Those who travel change," the duck says. "Your wish will have changed, too. You've become a different chicken, a better one. Other things have become more important to you."

"But what could possibly be more important to me?"

"Think about it," murmurs the duck, scratching the chicken gently behind the ear. "The answer might be looking you in the face."

"What's that?" asks the chicken.

"Only me—" breathes the duck.

"No." The chicken leaps up. "I mean what am I sitting on?"

She feverishly searches the ground, finds an oddly shaped stick, and feels it from all angles.

"Put that down," the duck snaps. "It's mine."

"Is that your crutch?" asks the chicken. "But how can it be? You left it in your backyard. How did it get to the top of the highest mountain in the world?"

The chicken's brain is rattling into action.

"Hang on. Something funny is going on here," she says. "I've thought so the whole time. A forest without trees, a river without water, a mountain without slopes. And the whole time we didn't meet another creature." She turns her head this way and that, listening.

"Where—am—I?"

The duck has a sudden lump in her throat. "Just let me explain," she says hoarsely. "You're still in my backyard, and we've been circling it—"

"What?!" The chicken is thunderstruck.

"Please don't get upset." The duck clears her throat, then the words tumble out. "I know you're angry, but really you ought to be grateful. The world out there is far too dangerous for a blind chicken. I've taken you under my wing and we've had many thrilling and incredible adventures behind these high walls. They didn't actually happen, but you surely admit you've never felt more alive."

Then the duck sighs. "You can speak now."

The chicken is silent. What can she possibly say? She can't find the words.

"Do you need time to calm down?" The duck  sobs quietly, just to be on the safe side. "Maybe you're afraid of saying something you'll regret later. But you can let rip and tell me how you feel. I can take it. Say whatever you like. But say something, please."

The chicken remains stubbornly silent. She is disappointed to the core. That duck can go on talking till her beak drops off, for all she cares.

"I know, I took it too far—"

The duck is wallowing in it.  "It's wrong to deceive a blind

chicken! There's no excuse for that. But I found I was having such fun. Especially with my death at the end. I can't go on like this, though. Punish me, please! Pluck out my feathers one by one! Roast me on a spit! But not speaking is the meanest thing you can do.

Please say something. Anything."

A grim silence from the chicken. She has nothing to say to this duck.

Not a word.

"You know what?" the duck bursts out. "You're stupid! You're so stupid it should be illegal! Did you seriously believe there's a place in the world where your secret wishes come true? That's completely implausible. Even if—"

The duck is flapping her wings with increasing agitation, and her feet lift off the ground. "Your wish will never come true. *Only happy if the whole world dances to your tune! That's megalomania!* Nobody has a right to rule anyone else. You're

nuts! A chicken like you ought to be locked up—"

The duck suddenly looks down. "What's going on? I'm flying! And it's easy! There's no great art to it—"

She flies higher and higher, flaps above the walls of her backyard, and sees the world from on high for the first time in her life.

What a sight!

She finally gets what is meant by a "bird's eye view." She shoots through the air with ease.

"I feel like—like—a rocket!"

In fact, the excited duck's voice can no longer be heard in the yard. Meanwhile, the blind chicken has seen the light.

"Are you still there?" she asks.

No reply.

"Are you still there?" she asks again. "I'm not the slightest bit angry anymore! Quite the opposite. What you did here in your backyard was like something out of the movies. I'd never have expected a dishrag duck to have such an imagination. You know what? I was having the time of my life. I just didn't realize it."

The chicken looks up and listens.

Silence.

"Where are you?" she cries in despair. "Come back! I have only one wish in the whole world." She opens her beak wide and squawks with all her might: "I want my duck back, my beloved ducky! I don't care about anything else!"

Her voice echoes around the backyard, and then silence falls again.

Dead silence.

An icy shiver runs down the chicken's spine as she realizes that she will be alone. Not just today or tomorrow, but forever.

For the rest of her life.

Her knees grow weak, and she'd sink to the ground if not for the crutch. She clasps it to her and vows never to let it go. This crutch is the only thing left of her ducky.

"You don't need a crutch," says a familiar voice. "You have me."

The chicken freezes.

"My wish! My wish has come true!" She stumbles towards the voice. "I thought I'd lost you forever, but you've come back, my beloved ducky—"

"My sunshine," says the duck. "I was only gone for a moment. Did you really think I'd leave you? I just went up for a quick look. The world out there isn't so dangerous after all. In fact, there

are all kinds of exciting things to discover. I think you'll love it. Come on!"

"But we're having such a nice friendly time in the yard," says the chicken. "Let's not talk for a little while and just enjoy the blissful silence. Anyway," she adds, "the world out there can't possibly be as wonderful as the one you created."

The chicken puts her wing around the duck's shoulders, turns her head this way and that, and breathes in the sweet smell of the backyard.

The duck soon tires of the silence. "Shall I tell you my secret wish now?"

"You don't have to." The chicken shakes her head. "Every duck has the right to a little secret. Anyway, I already know your secret wish. Right from the start, you've wanted me to stay with you forever." She squeezes the duck tightly. "You've hit the bullseye with me. Everyone loves me. It's not a crime. I go around spreading sunshine, and you—"

The chicken pauses.

"Go on," groans the duck.

"You," says the chicken, "are a true poet."

At these words, the duck goes pink beneath her feathers and once more is glad the chicken can't see it.

"You know what bothers me about you?" she asks softly.

"What?"

"Nothing."

This edition first published in 2022 by Gecko Press
PO Box 9335, Wellington 6141, New Zealand
info@geckopress.com

English-language edition © Gecko Press Ltd 2022
Translation © Helena Kirkby 2022

Copyright text and illustrations
© 2021 by CARLSEN Verlag GmbH, Hamburg, Germany
First published in Germany under the title *Lahme Ente, blindes Huhn*

Distributed in the United States and Canada by Lerner Publishing Group,
lernerbooks.com
Distributed in the United Kingdom by Bounce Sales and Marketing,
bouncemarketing.co.uk
Distributed in Australia and New Zealand by Walker Books Australia,
walkerbooks.com.au

Gecko Press is committed to sustainable practice. We publish books to be read
over and over. We use sewn bindings and high-quality production and print
all our new books on FSC-certified paper from sustainably managed forests.

Original language: German
Edited by Penelope Todd
Typesetting by Katrina Duncan
Printed in China by Everbest Printing Co. Ltd,
an accredited ISO 14001 & FSC-certified printer

ISBN hardback: 9781776574735
ISBN paperback: 9781776574728
Ebook available

For more curiously good books, visit geckopress.com

Gecko Press is a small-by-choice,
independent publisher of children's books
in translation. We publish a curated list
of books from the best writers
and illustrators in the world.

Gecko Press books celebrate unsameness.
They encourage us to be thoughtful and inquisitive,
and offer different—sometimes challenging, often
funny—ways of seeing the world. They are printed
on high-quality, sustainably sourced paper with
stitched bindings so they can be read and re-read.

For more Gecko Press illustrated chapter books,
visit our website or your local bookstore.
You might like...

Yours Sincerely, Giraffe by Megumi Iwasa
and Jun Takabatake, for readers who like receiving
letters and imagining things they've never seen.

Free Kid to Good Home by Hiroshi Ito, in which a
girl with a new potato-faced baby brother tries to
find a better family—and ends up happily back home.

Detective Gordon: The First Case by Ulf Nilsson
and Gitte Spee, for detective stories set in a friendly
forest, where Detective Gordon seeks justice for all
and always makes time for delicious cakes.

A Bear Named Bjorn by Delphine Perret, for readers
who enjoy a gentle bushwalk with an observant bear.